First published in Belgium and Holland by Clavis Uitgeverij, Hasselt – Amsterdam, 2014

English translation from the Dutch by Clavis Publishing Inc. New York

Visit us on the web at www.clavisbooks.com

The Princess of Shoes written and illustrated by Madelon Koelinga
Original title: *De Schoenenprinses*
Translated from the Dutch by Clavis Publishing

ISBN 978-1-60537-235-8

This book was printed in September 2015 at Publikum d.o.o., Slavka Rodica 6, Belgrade, Serbia

First Edition
10 9 8 7 6 5 4 3 2 1

Clavis Publishing supports the First Amendment and celebrates the right to read

The Princess of Shoes

Madelon Koelinga

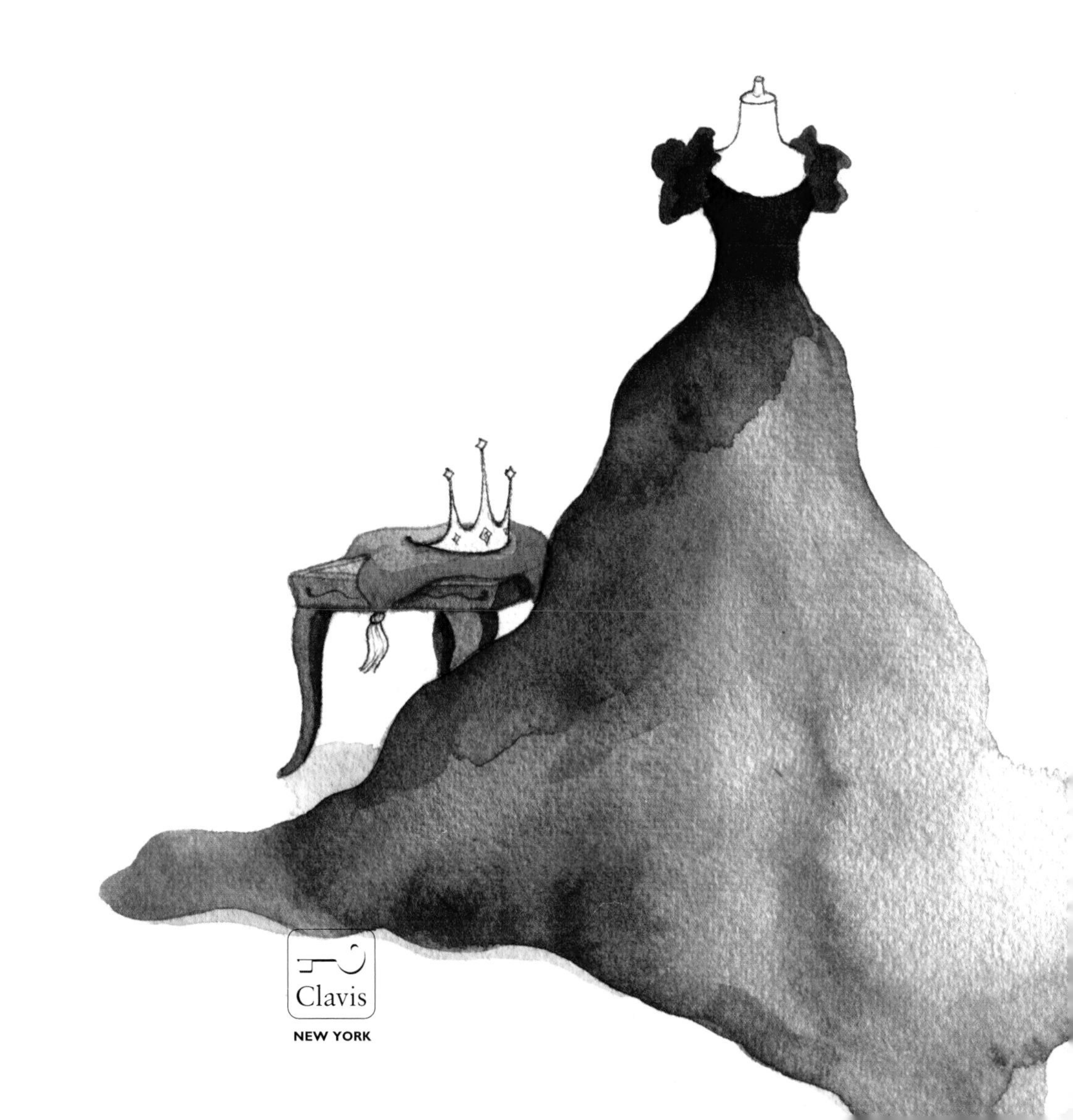

Clavis
NEW YORK

in a land far away, there was a princess.
Not just any princess!

Oh, no!

She was very **special.**

While other princesses
had to make do
with hundreds of shoes,
she had...

...thousands of them!

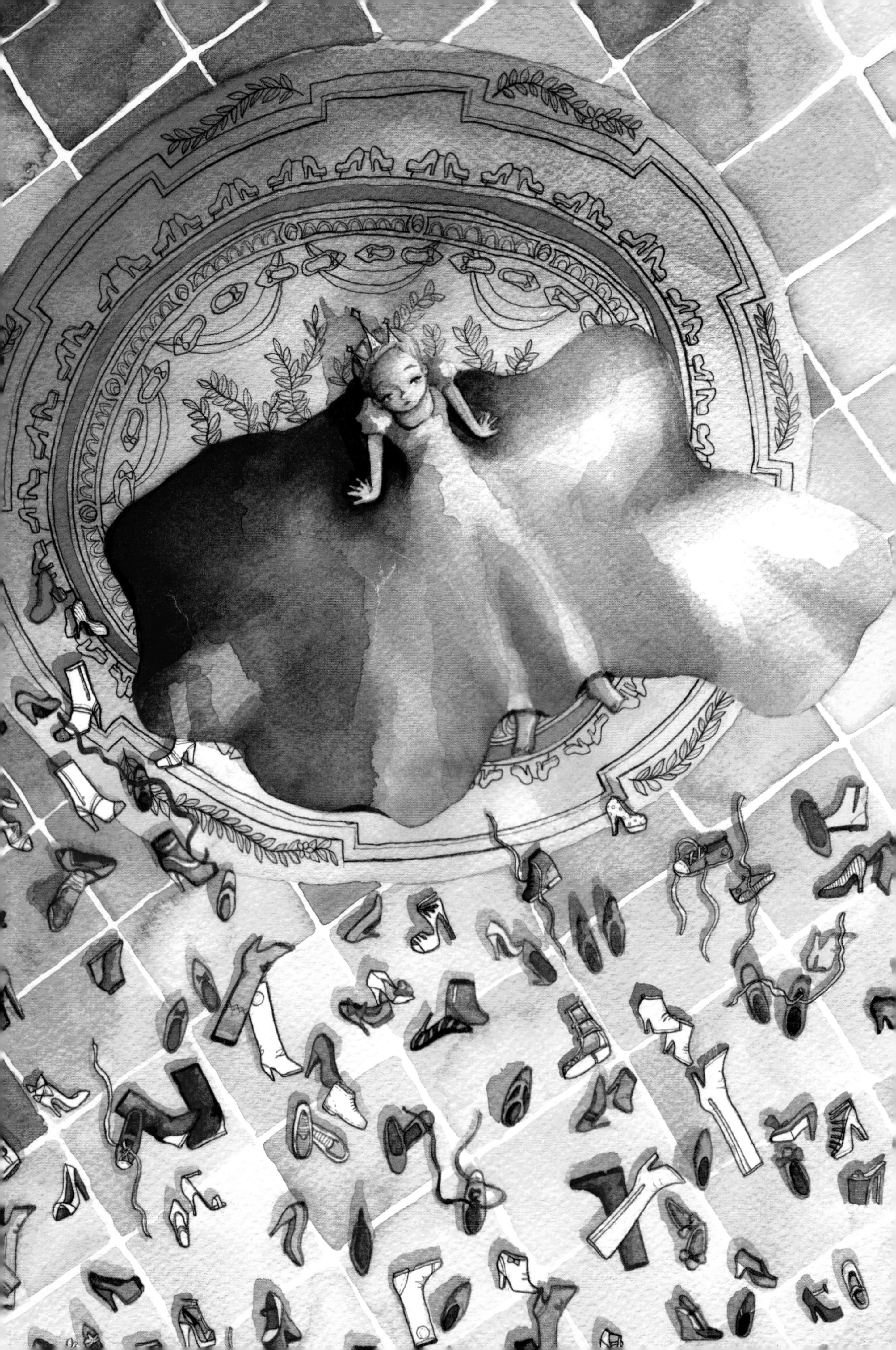

The princess could spend days and days in her room filled with shoes.

For every dress she owned,
she had **many pairs**
of shoes to match.

It was a pity that she couldn't wear
all her shoes at the same time but, well,
she had so many of them!

Even
with all those shoes,
the princess felt something
was missing.

She just didn't know **what....**

One day, when she was staring
out of the window,
she saw a woman walking by.

And not just **any** woman!

Oh, no! A woman wearing a pair of shoes
the princess had **never seen before.**

She couldn't believe her eyes.

She had to find out

where the woman had bought those shoes.

The princess ran out of her castle, onto the street and then towards the woman with the special shoes.

But when she got there,
the woman was **gone**.

The princess plunked herself down
by the edge of a fountain.

She was very upset that she hadn't been able
to find out where to get the shoes.

Then she heard a friendly voice
asking what was going on.
Behind her stood a girl she'd never seen before.
The princess explained her problem
and the girl offered to help her find the shoes.
The princess and the girl went around asking if anyone
had seen the stranger with the beautiful shoes.
They also checked all the stores.

After a while they got tired.
They took a break and while they rested
they talked about all sorts of things.

The princess couldn't remember
when last she'd had
such a good time.

The princess was enjoying herself so much
she almost forgot about the special shoes.

Then she noticed that her new friend
was wearing shoes that were old and scuffed.

And she wasn't the only one!

Suddenly the princess felt **ashamed**. She realized
that she had way more shoes than she needed.

She made a decision.

She asked her servants to collect her shoes and give them to the women in the village.

The women were happy
to have new shoes

and the princess made
lots of new friends.

And did she really give away **all** her shoes?

Oh, yes!

Well, almost all of them...